Hill Road
Country state
Downside
Sea view

Bill the Bat Loves Halloween

Written by Daryl K. Cobb

Illustrated by Manuela Pentangelo

10 To 2 Children's Books / Clinton

Library of Congress Control Number 2007929835

ISBN 978-1-4243-4454-3

Written by Daryl K. Cobb
Illustrated by Manuela Pentangelo

10 To 2 Children's Books

10to2childrensbooks.com

Printed in China

First Printing 2007

To my family - CC, KC and JC - for their continued support and inspiration.

Daryl K. Cobb

To my family and friends who support me every day, and to Daryl, for believing in me.

Happy Halloween to everyone!

Manuela Pentangelo

Bill the bat
loved Halloween.
It was the funniest thing
that he had ever seen.

The kids dressed up like ghouls and ghosts.

The boy called Nixon
scared him the most.

Bill spent the night
just flying
around.

To get a good look,
he had to swoop down.

The kids would all scream
and scatter away.
"A bat, a bat!"
he heard them all say.

Someone started a rumor
some years ago,

let me think, let me think,
now how did it go ?

A bat could swoop down
and get caught in your hair.

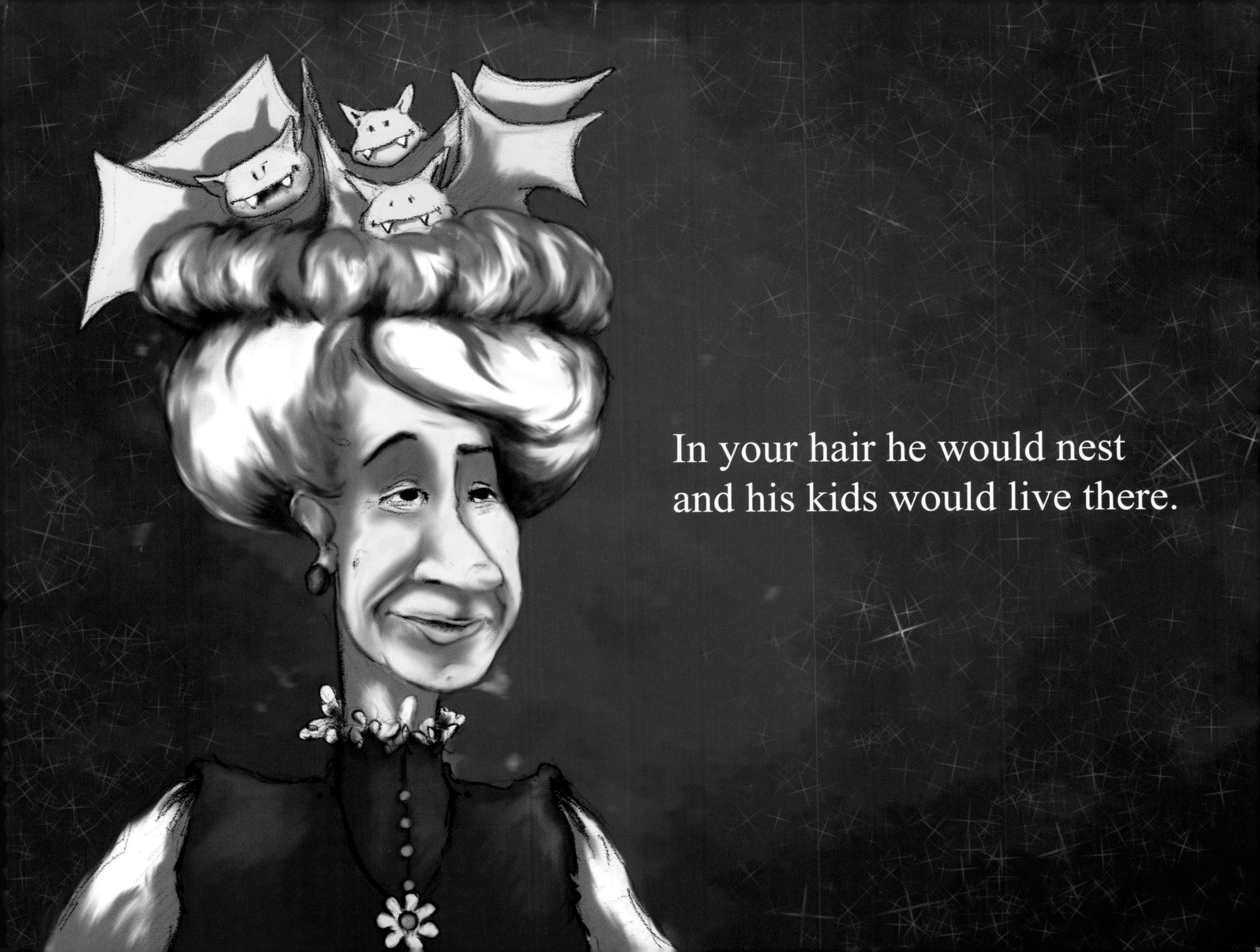

In your hair he would nest
and his kids would live there.

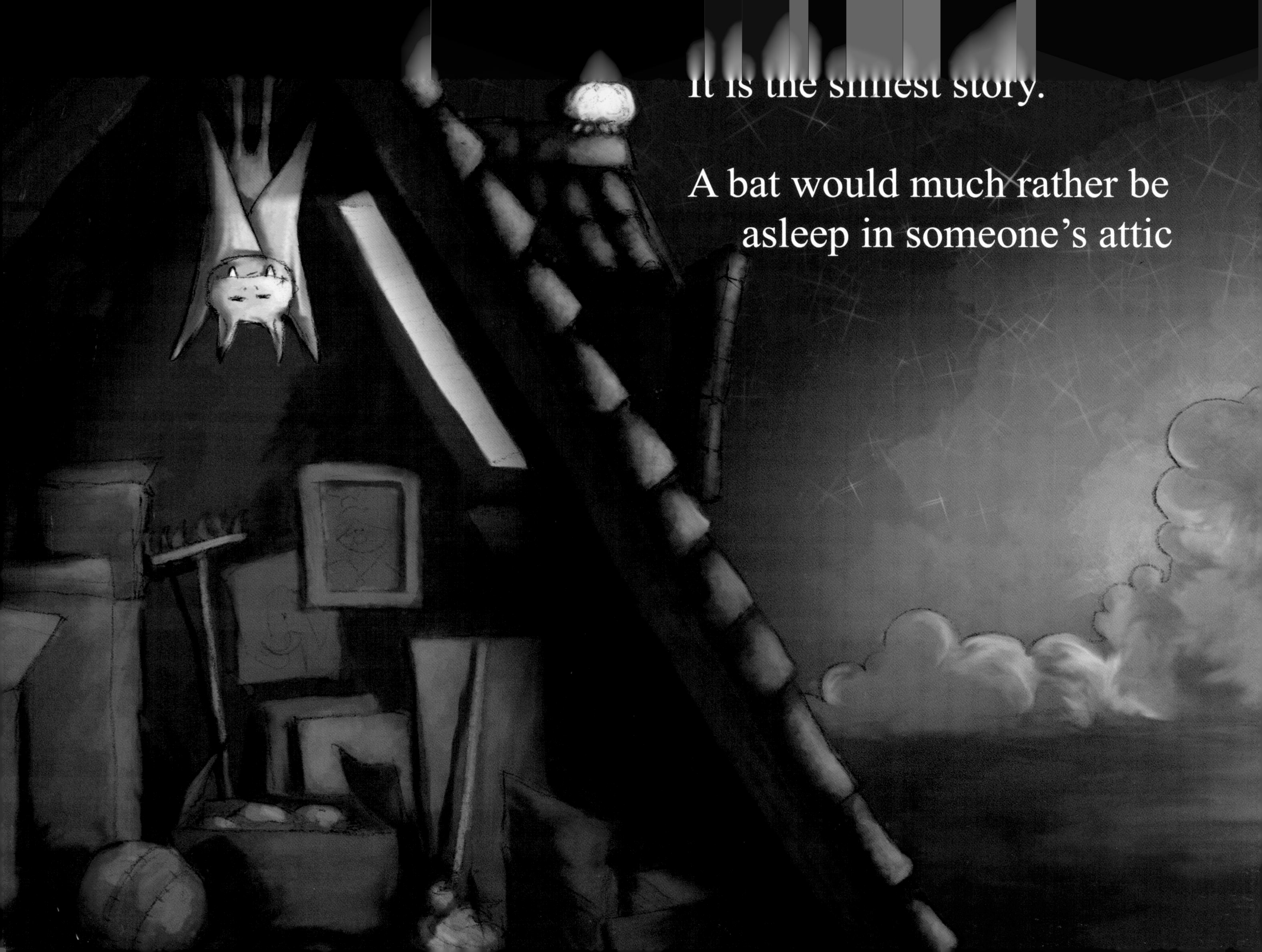
It is the silliest story.
A bat would much rather be
asleep in someone's attic

or in a cave by the sea.

But whatever the reasons,
the kids liked to run.
At this time of year,
to Bill this was fun.

THiS

He set himself down
on the branch of a tree,
to rest for a second

and what did he see?

The ghouls and the ghosts
on the porch of the house
and tagging along was
his friend Mike the mouse.

The moon was full,
the stars were bright,
the perfect setting
for a Halloween night.

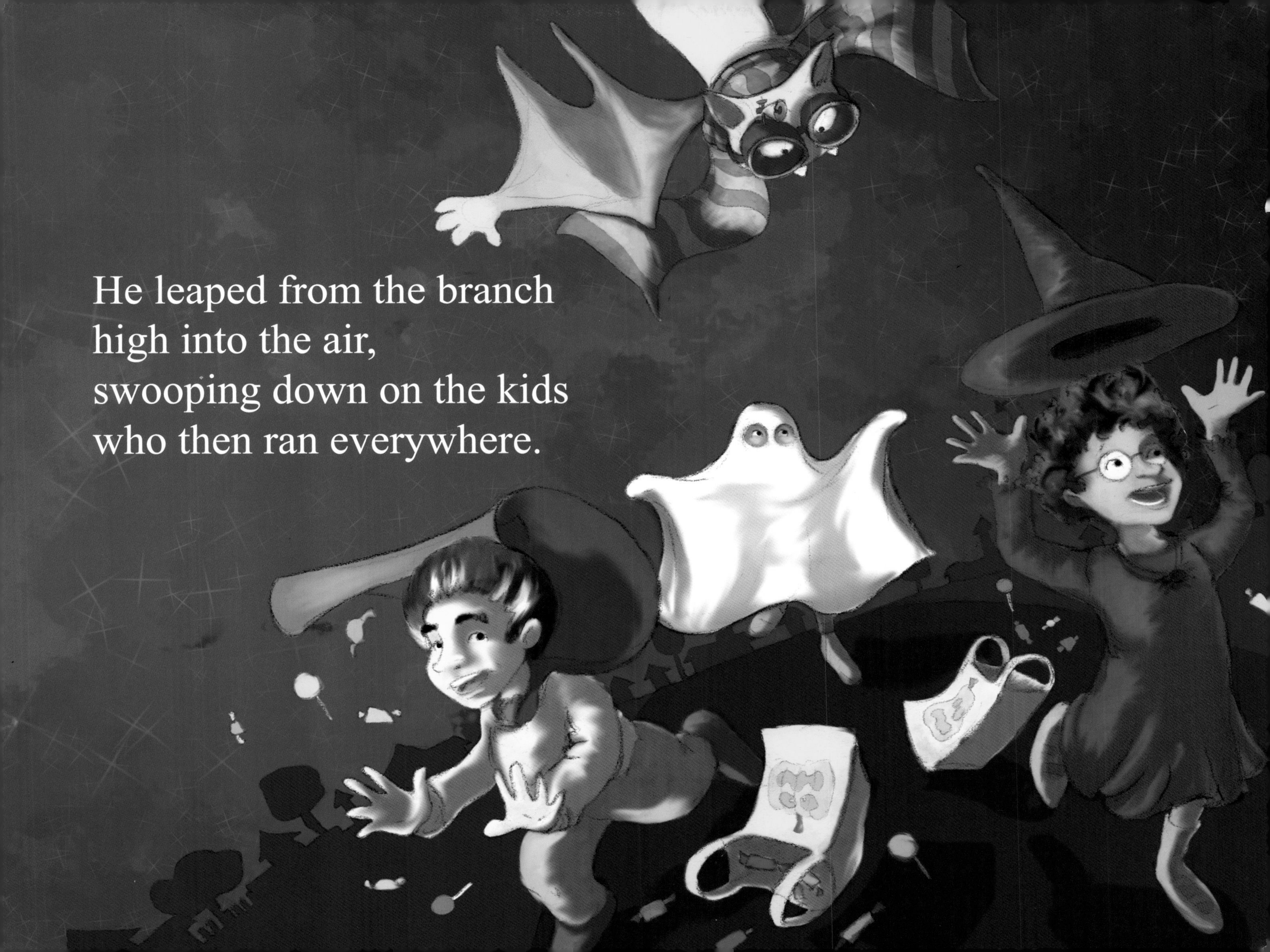

He leaped from the branch
high into the air,
swooping down on the kids
who then ran everywhere.

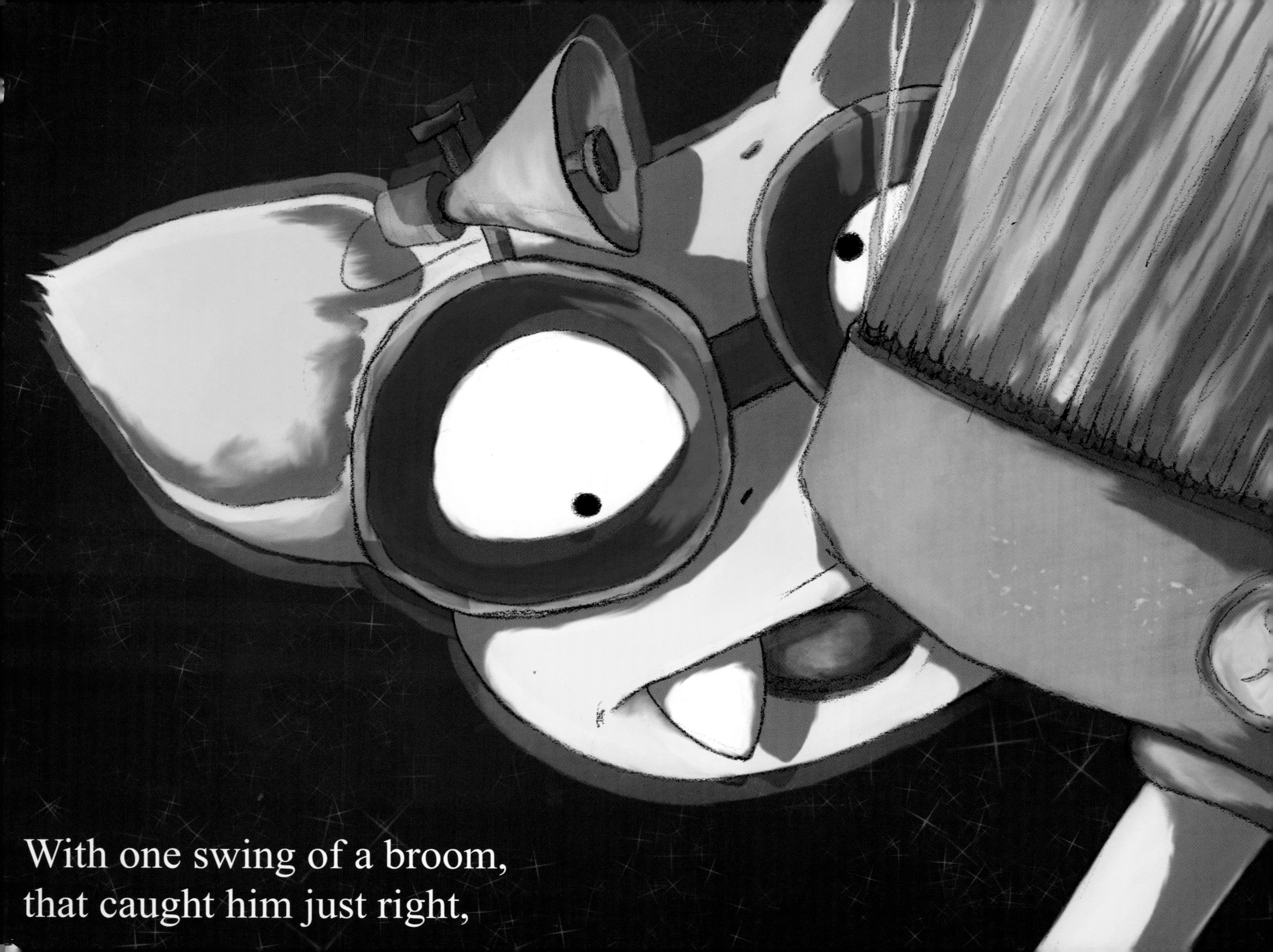

With one swing of a broom,
that caught him just right,

Bill was sent flying
back into the night.

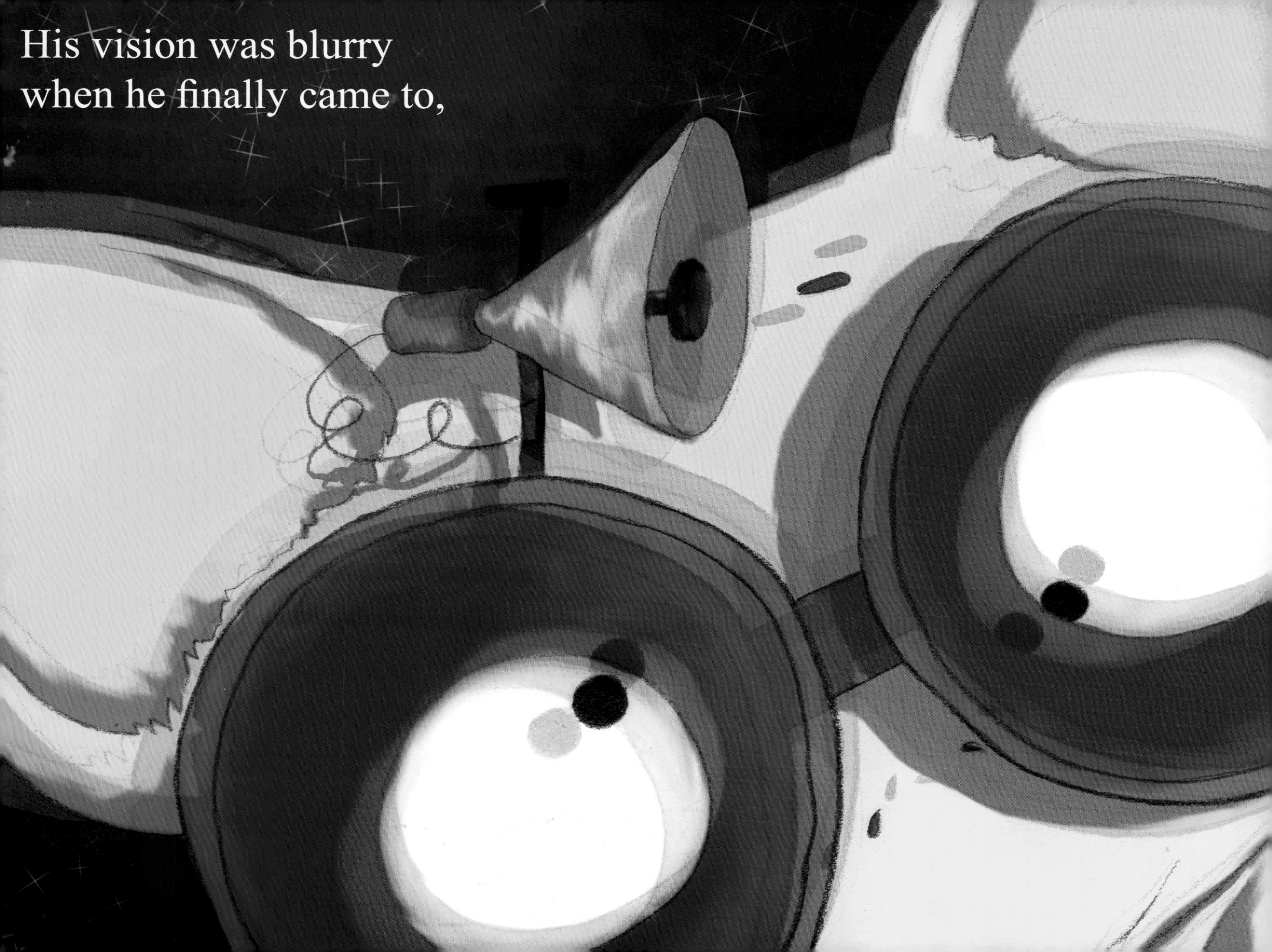

His vision was blurry
when he finally came to,

and Halloween night

was over, done, through.

Al the Owl from his perch
was shaking his head.
"I think you should
take up the tango," he said.

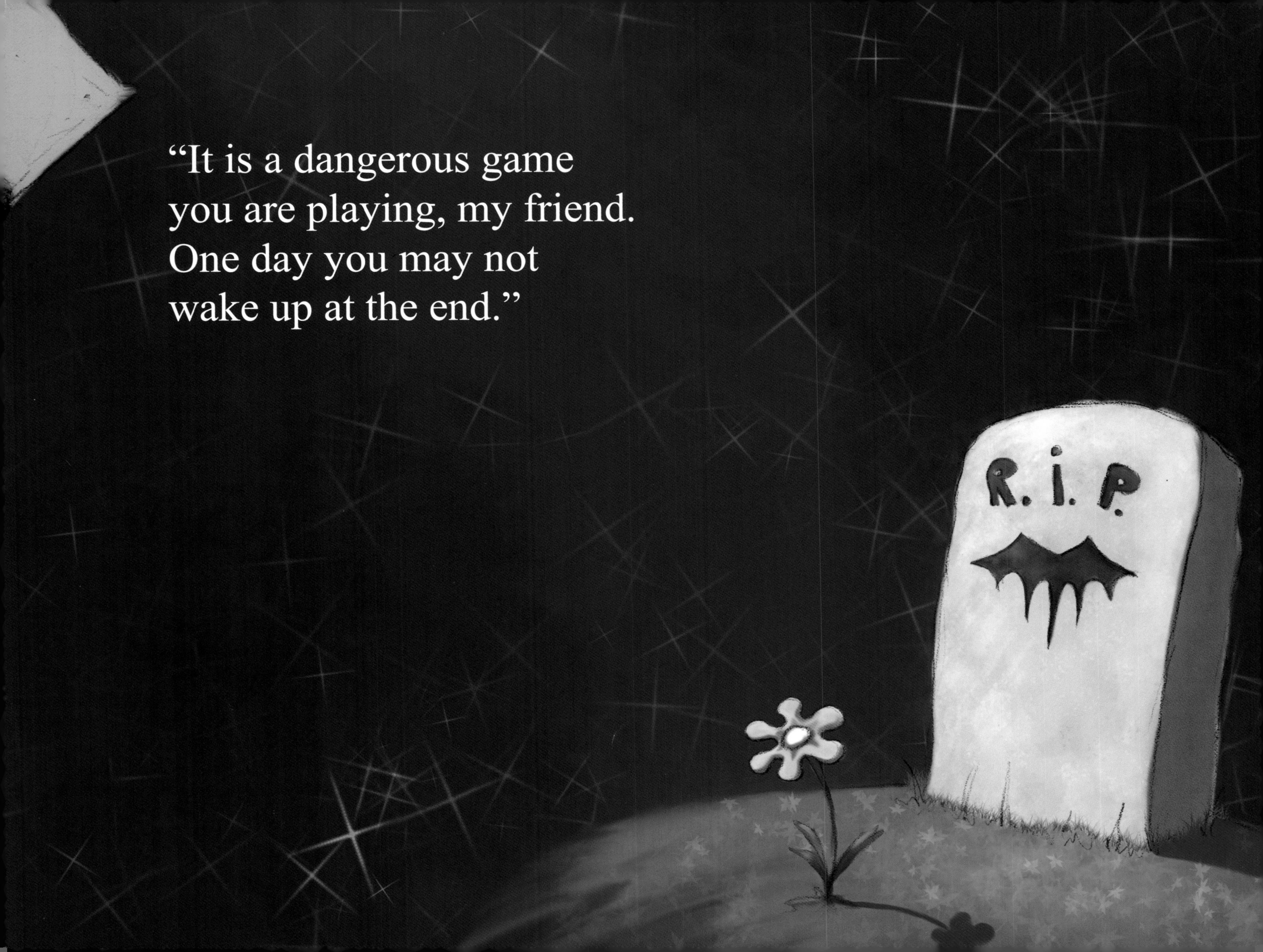

"It is a dangerous game
you are playing, my friend.
One day you may not
wake up at the end."

Bill thought for a moment,
"You are right, this is true.
Maybe next year
I'll just watch it with you."

The End